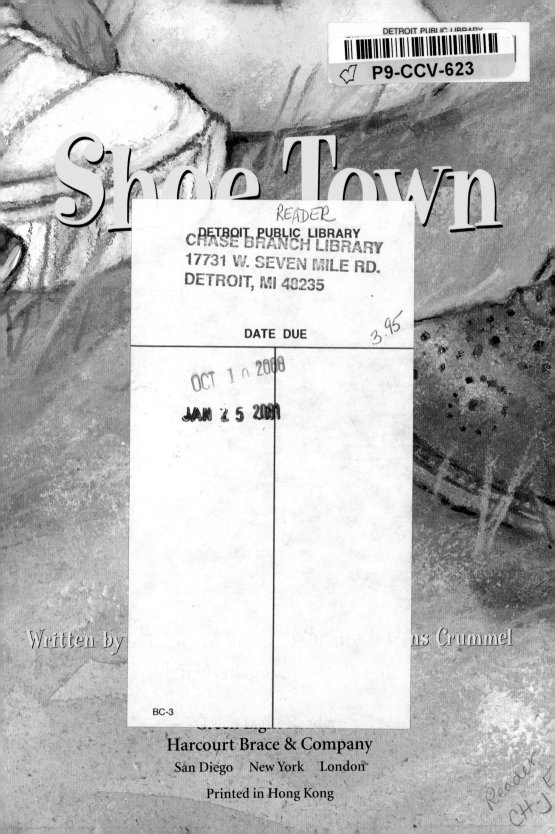

Shoe Town

Written by ... ns Crummel

Harcourt Brace & Company

San Diego   New York   London

Printed in Hong Kong

There was a little mouse
who had a little shoe.

When her babies grew up,
she knew just what to do.

"I'll fill a hot bath,
then I'll take a long nap."

Just then at her shoe
came a *rap-tap-tap-tap*.

"We are Tortoise and Hare.
We just went for a run.

Can we stay here with you . . .
in your shoe? Oh, what fun!"

"My shoe is too little
for so many to share.

Look for a shoe, if you please.
It can go over there."

"Now I'll fill a hot bath,
then I'll take a long nap."

Just then at her shoe
came a *rap-tap-tap-tap*.

"I'm the Little Red Hen.
And I love making bread.

Is there room in your shoe
for one more?" she said.

"My shoe is too little
for so many to share.

Look for a shoe, if you please.
It can go over there."

"Now I'll fill a hot bath,
then I'll take a long nap."

Just then at her shoe
came a big *RAP-TAP-TAP!*

"I'll huff and I'll puff
and I'll blow your shoes down—

if you don't let me stay
in your little shoe town!"

"Don't huff and don't puff.
We'll be happy to share.

Look for a shoe, if you please.
It can go over there."

More and more friends came.
The little town grew.

And to think it began
with a mouse and her shoe!

First Green Light Readers edition 1999
Green Light Readers is a trademark of Harcourt Brace & Company.

Library of Congress Cataloging-in-Publication Data
Stevens, Janet.
Shoe town/written by Janet Stevens and Susan Stevens Crummel;
illustrated by Janet Stevens.
p.   cm.
"Green Light Readers."
Summary: As she tries to settle down for a nap, a mouse who lives in a shoe is visited
first by Tortoise and Hare, then by Little Red Hen, and lastly by the Big Bad Wolf.
ISBN 0-15-201994-4
[1. Mice—Fiction. 2. Characters in literature—Fiction. 3. Shoes—Fiction.
4. Stories in rhyme.] I. Crummel, Susan Stevens. II. Title.
PZ8.3.S844Sh 1999
[E]—dc21   98-15564

A C E F D B

The illustrations in this book were done in watercolor crayon,
colored pencil, and watercolor with gesso on handmade paper.
The display type was set in Heatwave.
The text type was set in Minion.
Color separations by Bright Arts Ltd., Hong Kong
Printed by South China Printing Company, Ltd., Hong Kong
This book was printed on 140-gsm matte art paper.
Production supervision by Stanley Redfern and Ginger Boyer
Designed by Barry Age